Summary: Poetino takes us into his life—sharing people, places, things, and his Italian culture with warmth, sensitivity, and humor.

ISBN: 978-0-615-36873-3

[1. Family-Fiction; 2. Diversity-Fiction; 3. Friendship-Fiction; 4. Education-Fiction; 5. Italian Americans-Fiction]

J.M. Giusti-Gambini Publishing, LLC
7259 Creeks Bend Court
West Bloomfield, Michigan 48322

www.poetino.com
www.jmgiusti-gambinipublishing.com

Ciao, I Am Poetino

By Josephine Gambini
Illustrated by Jordan Stafford

J.M. Giusti-Gambini Publishing, LLC

Dedication

To Mamma, Giuditta Giusti-Gambini,
for Poetino,

to Papa, Carlo Gambini,
for loving Giuditta so very much,

to my niece, Danielle Goaley,
for loving Poetino as much as I do, and

to my sister, Carla Gambini-Goaley,
for giving us Danielle.

Ciao! I am **Poetino**. You ask, how did I get my **nome**?

When **Mamma** held me in her arms at the hospital, she looked at me with great love and said, "You are my little poet. **Sì**, you look like a little Italian poet, and so you shall be named **Poetino**."

Even **Papà** was surprised, but he said, "I like it! **Sì**, he does have the look of a poet. Who knows? Maybe someday he will be a poet!"

I live with **Mamma**, **Papà**, and my big **sorella**, Danielle; we call her Dani, and my **fratellino**, Benjamin, whom we call Benny. We have a **cane** whose name is Charlie; he is master of our **casa**. I love my **famiglia** and they really love me, even when I am naughty!

We are Italian with just a little bit of Irish. But we are American, too, because my **nonni**, **Nonna Giuditta** and **Nonno Carlo**, migrated from Italy and became American citizens. They are **Mamma's** mom and dad. **Papà's** mom and dad, **Nonna Camilla** and **Nonno Lorenzo**, live in Italy. We will visit them soon.

I live in San Francisco. They call San Francisco "the **città** by the Bay". Sometimes people call it Frisco. **Papà** says the city is a peninsula because it is surrounded on three sides by water. I think it is a very beautiful city. **Nonna** calls it "**una bella città**." We have two big bridges, the Golden Gate and the Bay Bridge, which has two levels, an upper and lower level.

I love the hills in San Francisco. Sometimes **Papà** drives us up and down the hills, and I feel like I am on a roller coaster.... Wheee!

Dani is an ice skater. She lives to skate. She is very, very good at ice skating and does all kinds of spins and jumps. I like to watch her skate because she reminds me of a **cigno** as she glides across the rink. She never seems to get tired or dizzy from the spins. She never even gets hurt from the big jumps. She just knows how to do everything. She is really cool! Of course, she practices, practices, practices....

Dani usually comes in **prima** in ice skating competitions; if not **prima**, **seconda**. **Nonna** always says, "**Brava mia Daniela**," as **Nonno** smiles with pride. Dani's eyes are **verdi** just like the **occhi** of a **gatto**. **Papà** says her **occhi verdi** come from his side of the family. He says he is one-third Irish and two-thirds Italian. **Papà** says she has Irish **occhi**.

Sometimes I make Dani angry. I am mischievous and hide her skates when she has to go to practice at the rink. She says, "**Poetino**, if you don't get my skates, I will skin you alive!" I know she will not. I, also, know when Dani means business and so I get the skates for her. She looks at me with a scowl which says, "I am **arrabbiata**!" I laughingly get out of her way. I know she will get over it.

In fact, she always is our protector, Benny's and mine. She defends me when kids tease me about my **nome** and funny **orecchi**.

Dani gets all A's in **scuola**. **Mamma** says she is very smart, and she is in the Honors Program at **scuola**. She received an award last year at the Science Fair for her science project. She helps Benny and me whenever we need help.

I play ice hockey because I, too, love skating. I learned to skate from Dani.

I like to ride with Quinton as he clears the ice on the resurfacing machine. It is really cool!

Papà is always helping me with my homework and ice hockey. He comes to all my hockey games and tells me I am doing well. This makes me feel **bravo**. When he helps me with homework, he sometimes says, "**Poetino**, you are not focusing. You need to focus." He says focusing is important in hockey, too. **Papà** is very patient with me.

Papà likes my drawings. He says maybe I'll be **un poeta e un artista**. And maybe I will! I love to draw, and he always asks me about the things I draw. I very much like to draw **alberi**. They have a magic about them. **Papà** says focus is also important in drawing. **Papà** is an architect. He, too, likes to draw.

Mamma is perfect. Even **Papà** says this. I love everything she does for us because she makes everything fun. I love her cooking, especially **ravioli**. **Mamma** and **Nonna** get together every holiday and make lots of **ravioli** so we can feast on them. They are always saying, "**Mangia**!"

Dani likes to help **Mamma** in the kitchen. **Mamma** says she is a good **cuoca**. Dani makes really good **lasagna**. It is as good as **Mamma's**, even **Mamma** says so! **Nonna** says "**È una brava cuoca, Daniela.**"

Mamma likes to write stories, and she lets me draw pictures for them. I love to do this. **Mamma** likes to read the stories to us. I also write stories, and **Mamma** lets me read them to her. She tells me that maybe I will be **un poeta e un artista**. And maybe I will!

Mamma is a **maestra**. She loves teaching because she loves her **studenti**. **Mamma** also helps me with my homework. Both **Mamma** and **Papà** teach me Italian. I like speaking Italian, especially with my **nonna** and **nonno**.

Mamma does get **arrabbiata** with me and sends me to my room when I tease Benny and take away his **giocattoli** so he can't find them.

Benny is a big baby sometimes. He tries to get me into trouble. When he spills things, breaks them, or misplaces his **giocattoli**, he blames me. And because I am older, **Mamma** says, "**Poetino**, you better shape up and stop bothering Benny."

But most of the time Benny and I play together with our **treni** and planes.

I like to take him to the **parco** with me and my buddies to play basketball. He is my little buddy. Benny's **occhi** are **blu**, just like **Papà's**. My **occhi** are **marroni**, just like **Mamma's**.

Charlie is our **cane**; he is lots of fun. He is my **cane**. He is a collie and is **marrone** and **bianco**. He looks like Lassie! **Papà** bought him when I was little because I wanted a dog. **Nonno** says, "**Charlie è bello, intelligente, e divertente**." He obeys us most of the time. He usually sleeps with me. Sometimes when I ignore him because I am playing with my **amici**, he sleeps with Benny instead of me. **Mamma** says even dogs get their feelings hurt when they are ignored. They are a lot like people.

Benny and I usually walk him, but sometimes Dani and **Papà** do. I love Charlie; so do my **amici**. He comes to the **parco** with us and we play fetch the ball. He loves me, too.

My best buddies are Sammy, Ralphy, Jordan, and Chiu. Sammy gets good grades, like A's in all his subjects. The teachers say he is gifted. He helps Ralphy and me when we have trouble with math. I sometimes have trouble focusing. I get distracted, but with **Mamma's**, **Papà's**, and Dani's help, I am getting better. Chiu is learning disabled, but he is getting help and is also doing better. Sammy and I are good hockey players. Jordan and Chiu like to run. They are on the track team. We are true friends.

Jordan loves to draw, like I do. He and I work on art **scuola** projects together. It is so cool!

My **amici** and I have lots of fun. We love to explore new things and investigate new **posti**. We play ice hockey and go to **scuola** together. We live in the same neighborhood in San Francisco. We go to the **parco** and play ball. We bike and swim together, but mainly we just talk. There is always a lot to talk about—important things and not so important things. We talk about what we will do when we grow up and what we will do the next day. We play video games, too.

Sometimes my **amici** and I go to the movies with Dani and her **amica**, Rebecca; Rebecca skates with Dani. Benny comes with us sometimes. We like action movies, spy movies, and movies with lots of technology in them.

Sometimes we get into trouble, like when we ordered pizza to be delivered to Mr. Dreary across the street. We watched him go to the door and argue with the delivery boy. Mr. Dreary was really **arrabbiato**! Somehow he knew we did it. We got into big trouble! **Mamma** sent me to my room, and **Papà** had me save all my allowance until I saved enough money to pay Mr. Dreary for the pizza. We all had to apologize to Mr. Dreary. We really felt bad.

I like school, but some days are better than others. Usually the bad days are bad because I did not do my homework or we have a test. Tests make me nervous. The **maestra**, Ms. Desmond, also gets upset when I am daydreaming, not paying attention, or talking when I should be listening. She, too, says I need to focus. But Ms. Desmond is **brava**. She makes us work and wants us to do well. And she knows when to give me the look, or to say "**Poetino**" in a serious tone so I will straighten up and get busy. She is fair and makes **scuola** fun. I like her a lot.

I like to read and write. But I also like social studies because we study about people like gladiators and warriors, and **posti**, like Africa and Italy. I hope to go to those **posti** some day and lots of other **posti**, too.

I like science when we do experiments, like seeing molecules move; my favorite experiment is the one where we use sulfur and practically choke from the smell of rotten eggs. It is really cool!

My **tata** is a maestra like **Mamma**. She, too, loves her **studenti** at the university where she is a professor. She lives in Michigan. **Tata** loves to travel and goes to all kinds of **posti**. She says she is going to take us with her when we get older. I cannot wait!

We can't wait to see **Tata** when she returns from her trips. She collects **bambole** for Dani, **treni** for Benny, and t-shirts for me.

Tata comes to our special events and activities whenever she can. And when she visits, she takes us to the zoo, concerts, aquarium, and the science museum. She even plays hide-and-seek with us. She can never find us. She has as much fun as we do. **Nonna** says, "**Tata** is always in motion."

Two of my very, very favorite people are my **Nonna Giuditta** and **Nonno Carlo**. **Nonna** is special. She tells us wonderful stories in Italian. We could listen for hours. She is also the best **cuoca** ever. Everyone loves to go to **Nonna** and **Nonno's** house.

Nonno is a great gardener. Everyone in the neighborhood says **Nonno's giardino** is **bello**. It has lots of **fiori**—calla lilies, roses, irises, and many others. He has a big orange tree and a lemon tree in the garden and shares **limoni** and **aranci** with his neighbors. He also grows lots of herbs in the **giardino**—sage, rosemary, parsley, and more. **Nonna** uses the herbs when she cooks. We love the vegetables he grows—like tomatoes, zucchini, string beans, and squash. They are delicious! **Nonna** says, "**Il giardino è molto bello**." **Nonno** and **Nonna** love Italy; they love America, too. They speak mainly in Italian but some English, too.

In the summer, Dani, Benny, Charlie, and I spend a month with **Nonno** and **Nonna** at their cottage in the country. It is north of San Francisco, across the Golden Gate Bridge in the wine country. It is a special place. There are all kinds of fruit trees at my **nonni's** cottage. We pick peaches, apricots, and apples right off the **alberi**. They are yummy.

Nonno and **Nonna** take us swimming in the Russian River which flows through the town. We have picnics on the river, roast marshmallows, tell stories, and sing to our hearts' content. We have a great time! We go to barbecues with **Nonno** and **Nonna**, and they play games with us.

In the fall, usually in **settembre** or **ottobre**, we all go to our **nonni's** cottage to pick grapes. **Nonno** says this is the **vendemmia**. Beautiful grape vines cover the earth. At this time, the grapes are ready for picking, and the vines are a carpet of **rosso**, **arancio**, and **oro**. It is a magical ride of color to our **nonni's** cottage. **L'uva** is **buona**, too.

The whole **famiglia** picks **l'uva**. We have a big **festa,** and then **Nonno** makes **vino**. We call him the "Little Old Wine Maker." He always shares **uva** and **vino** with his **amici**.

It is always an Italian **festa** at my **nonni's casa**. Even when we break something, she scolds us gently but always says, "It is only a thing, but you are precious." And that is how she makes us feel. Sometimes when we get too silly, my **nonna** says, "**Basta**!" Then we quiet down. I love my **Nonno Carlo**, too.

Nonno sings great Italian songs, even opera. He is always entertaining us at our parties, like when it's our **compleanno** or **Natale**. **Nonno** teaches me how to play Italian card games like **scopa**. **Nonno** and **Nonna** immigrated to America from Lucca, Italy.

What I love most is when I leave **Nonna**, she says "**Ciao**," to everyone and then always says to me, "**Ciao, Poetino, mio bambino.**"

My very best **amico** is my **topolino bianco**, named **Poetino Piccolino**, who lives with me in my room in a special **gabbia** with **giocattoli**. I talk with **Poetino Piccolino**, and he always listens and nods. **Poetino Piccolino** became part of my life when I was very sick.

My **Nonna Giuditta** told me that once when she was little and got very sick in Italy, she found a little **topolino bianco**. **Nonna** took it and made it a little **casa** with a **scatola**. She loved it and it became the best pet ever! I asked **Nonna** if I could have a **topolino bianco** for a pet, and she got me **Poetino Piccolino**. She thought **Poetino Piccolino** would be a perfect name. He is the best pet ever! I love **Poetino Piccolino**.

Here comes **Mamma** and **Papà**.
"**Poetino**, time for bed. Have you finished your story?"
"**Sì, Mamma**. Tomorrow I shall read it to you."
"Good. Say your prayers, and then lights out."
"Ok, **Mamma**."
"**Buona notte, Poetino**."

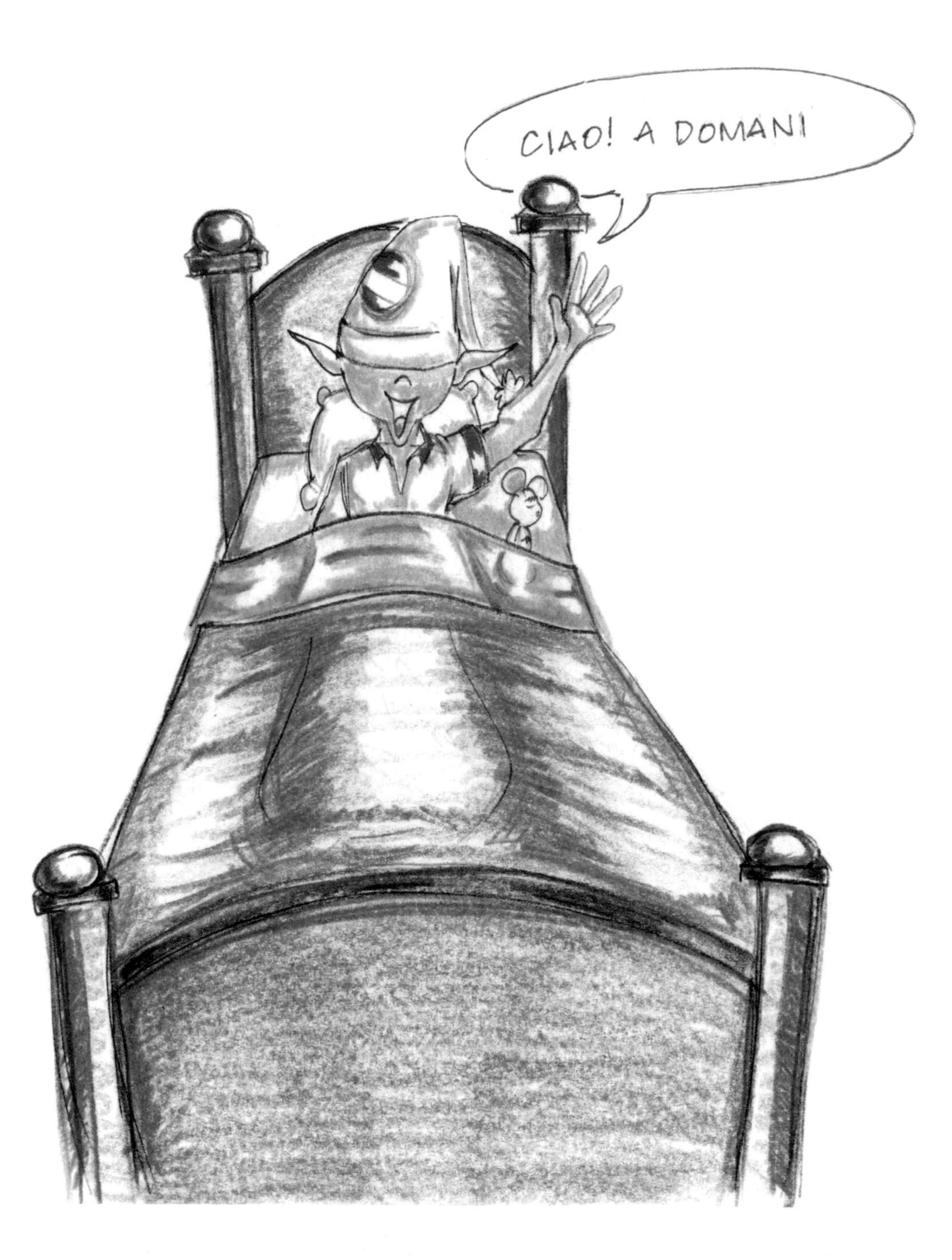

"Buona notte, Mamma, Papà. Buona notte, Charlie and **Poetino Piccolino. Ciao a domani!"**

Poetino's Italian Word Power

A

alberi	ahl beh ree	trees
amici (o) (a)	ah mee chee (ko) (ka)	friends (boy/girl friend)
aranci (o)	ah rahn chee (cho)	oranges (color orange)
arrabbiato (a)	ahr rhab bee yiah toh (tah)	angry
artista	ahr tee stah	artist

B

bambino	bahm bee noh	little boy
bambole	bahm boh lah	dolls
basta	bahs tah	enough
bello (a)	behl loh (lah)	handsome (beautiful)
bianco	bee ahn koh	white
blu	bloo	blue
bravo (a)	brah voh (vah)	good; skilled boy (girl)
buona	boo oh nah	good; tasty

C

Camilla	kah meel lah	Camille
cane	kah neh	dog
Carlo	kar lo	Charles; Charlie
casa	kah zah	house
ciao	chee ah oh	hi; hello; goodbye
cigno	cheen yoh	swan

città	cheet tah	city
compleanno	kohm pleh ahn noh	birthday
cuoca	koo oh kah	cook
D		
Daniela	dah nee yiel lah	Danielle
divertente	dee ver ten teh	fun
domani	doh mah nee	tomorrow
E		
e	eh	and
è	eh	is
F		
famiglia	fah mee lyah	family
festa	feh stah	party
fiori	fee oh ree	flowers
fratellino	frah tehl lee noh	little brother
G		
gabbia	gahb bee ah	cage
gatto	gaht toh	cat
giardino	jahr dee noh	garden
giocattoli	joh kaht toh lee	toys
Giuditta	jee yew dit tah	Judith

I

il	eel	the
intelligente	in tel lee jen teh	intelligent

L

lasagna	lah sahn nyah	layered pasta
limoni	lee moh nee	lemons
Lorenzo	loh ren zoh	Lawrence

M

maestra	mah eh strah	teacher
Mamma	mahm mah	mama; mom
mangia	mahn jah	eat
marroni(e)	mah roh nee (neh)	brown
mio (a)	mee oh (ah)	mine, my (girl)
molto	mohl toh	very

N

Natale	nah tah leh	Christmas
nome	no meh	name
nonni (o) (a)	nohn nee (noh) (nah)	grandparents (father) (mother)
notte	noht teh	night

O

occhi	oh kee	eyes
orecchi	oh ray kee	ears
oro	oh roh	gold

ottobre	oht toh breh	October
P		
papà	pah pah	papa; dad
parco	pahr koh	park
piccolino	peek koh lee noh	little; small
poeta	poh eh tah	poet
poetino	poh eh tee noh	little poet
posti	poh stee	places
prima	pree mah	first
R		
ravioli	rah vee oh lee	Italian dumplings
rosso	rohs soh	red
S		
scatola	scah toh lah	box
scopa	skoh pah	broom/sweep card game
scuola	skoo oh lah	school
seconda	seh kon dah	second
settembre	seht tehm breh	September
sì	see	yes
sorella	sor rayl lah	sister
studenti	stu den tee	students

T

tata	tah tah	aunt (term of endearment)
topolino	toh poh lee noh	little mouse
treni	tray nee	trains

U

un; una	oon; oo nah	a, an, one
l'uva; uva	loo va; oo va	the grapes; grapes

V

vendemmia	ven dem mee ah	harvest of the grapes
vino	vee noh	wine
verdi	vayr dee	green

Translation - Sentences and Phrases

1. **Brava mia Daniela.**	Good my Danielle.
2. **Buona notte.**	Good night.
3. **Charlie è bello, intelligente e divertente.**	Charlie is beautiful, intelligent and fun.
4. **Ciao, a domani.**	Goodbye until tomorrow.
5. **Ciao, Poetino, mio bambino.**	Goodbye, Poetino, my little boy.
6. **È una brava cuoca, Daniela.**	Danielle is a good cook.
7. **Il giardino e molto bello.**	The garden is very beautiful.
8. **un poeta e un artista**	a poet and an artist
9. **una bella città**	a beautiful city

About the Author

The daughter of Italian immigrants, Josephine Gambini knows and appreciates the Italian language and revels in first-hand Italian experience. Her Italian heritage has greatly influenced her life and work. She is an educator and a psychologist, who taught at the university for thirty-four years and maintained a clinical practice. She is a native of San Francisco and relocated to the Detroit metro area where she presently resides.

Although she has written extensively for academia, this is her first children's book—and a dream fulfilled—to bring **Poetino** and those he loves to life, so they may be enjoyed by children and adults.

About the Illustrator

Jordan Stafford is an African-American student at Saginaw Valley State University. He is majoring in art and business. He resides in Detroit. He has been involved in both the visual and performing arts in his community and at his high school, Loyola High School, prior to attending the university. This is the first book he has illustrated. He is able to capture **Poetino** and those he loves with a joy that brings the characters to life.

Acknowledgments

Robert Blanchard
Nancy Gibney
Katherine Gross
Heather Hajduk
Karen Hickman
Susan Homant
Angela Knight
Charlotte Maloney
David Mastrangelo, SJ
Laudomia Merli-Blanchard
Jeanne Morgan
Paul Morgan
Antwoin Mosely
Karen Shirilla
Arnold Stafford
Audrey Stafford
Jonathan Stafford
Kumar Tuft

Poetino Piccolino Saves the Day—Coming Soon!